About This Book

SIDEWALK STORY
by Sharon Bell Mathis

Lilly Etta couldn't wait for her new gold earrings. Her mother had promised her a pair and her best friend, Tanya, was going to help pick them out. But something strange was going on at Tanya's house. Who were those men going into Tanya's apartment? Lilly Etta's mother wouldn't let her go over to Tanya's, which could mean only one thing. Tanya's family was being evicted. But not if Lilly Etta had anything to say about it! The city didn't care about Tanya's family, but Lilly Etta did, and she was going to make sure that her best friend did not leave without a fight.

Sidewalk Story

SHARON BELL MATHIS

ILLUSTRATED BY LEO CARTY

For my mother
Alice Frazier Bell
and my daughters
Sherie, Stacy, & Stephanie

Published by The Trumpet Club
1540 Broadway, New York, New York 10036

ISBN 0-440-84863-6

This edition published by arrangement with Viking Penguin, a division of
Penguin Books USA Inc.
Set in Janson
Printed in the United States of America
January 1992

3 5 7 9 10 8 6 4 2
CWO

Lilly Etta Allen, your ears look a mess, all sore and red! How you think these straws going to keep the holes open when you keep messing with them? Huh?"

"I wish my birthday would hurry up and get here. I *hate* these ugly straws! I just hate them!"

"Hold still. You'll get real gold earrings for your birthday—if you're good. I'm saving money, fast as I can."

"Phooey," Lilly Etta said. "Phooey!"

"There. The straws are back in."

"*Phooey!*" Lilly Etta said again.

"Go on outside and sit on the stoop or something. I don't want you far away when the twins wake up— I might need you to help me."

"You mean I can't go to the park?"

"I mean you can't go to the park."

"How come?"

"You can't go today."

"Phooey." Lilly Etta made a face but her mother didn't see it.

"Lilly Etta, you say 'phooey' one more time today and you won't ever get those real gold earrings. I'm tired of hearing you say that word. If you're going out, you better go now! One more 'phooey' and you stay in!"

Lilly Etta opened the front door of her apartment and walked out into the long hallway.

"And don't *touch* your ears. You hear me?"

"Phooey," Lilly Etta said in her smallest voice. "Phooey, phooey, phooey. And phooey some more!"

There were thirty-six steps down to the outside door, which led to the street, and each of the steps had a squeak. Because Lilly Etta was angry she said "Phooey" on each step. It sounded like phooey-squeak, phooey-squeak. Phooey. Phooey. Phooey. Squeak! Squeak! Squeak!

She jumped the last two steps, yanked the front door open, plunked herself down on the wide brownstone steps, and leaned against the heavy-looking black metal railing. She touched her ears. "I'm never going to get real gold earrings. Never!"

2

Just then a large truck stopped in front of the apartment building next door. Somebody's moving, Lilly Etta thought. "Who's moving?" she yelled to the workmen who climbed from the truck and went toward the building. But they ignored her.

A shiny black car drove up and stopped behind the truck. Two men, not dressed like the workmen, got out. They wore dark suits and ties and sparkling white shirts. But their faces had no sparkle as they walked quickly into the building behind the workmen.

Other children and a few grownups watched the men. Some of the grownups were whispering. As the men disappeared into the building a man yelled at them from across the street. "Go back where you came from. Nobody needs you around here!"

Lilly Etta stared at him and forgot she wanted to go to the park. Something was wrong. What did the man mean?

Now the man was talking to Eddie's father. Eddie's father was listening and looking across to the building. Lilly Etta knew by the frowns on their faces that something wasn't too cool.

One of the workmen came out of the building and

got some heavy ropes from the truck. Then he went back into the building. Lilly Etta thought of the workmen who had moved her family. Those men were fun. They had laughed and fooled around and smiled. Lilly Etta had gotten a chance to ride down on every chair—until her mother found out. After that, she got no more rides on the furniture.

This workman didn't look happy at all. She watched him come back for some more ropes. Somebody *must* be moving—but who?

When the workmen came out of the building carrying some yellow chairs, Lilly Etta stood up. "That's Tanya's stuff," she yelled. "Tanya's my best friend. She can't move! She didn't tell me she was moving!"

Lilly Etta ran down from her stoop and up to the stoop next door. "Tanya! Tanya!"

The men were bringing out more furniture. "Move, little girl," one of them said. "Move out the way."

Lilly Etta was trying to squeeze past them when she heard her mother calling. "Lilly Etta? Lilly Etta?"

Lilly Etta backed out of the hallway, ran down the stone steps to the street, and looked up. "Here I am. I didn't go anywhere. Tanya's moving and I want to go see her and help or something!"

"Come upstairs."

"Can't I stay here and watch? Maybe Tanya will come out. Please?"

"Come upstairs. I need you to help me." Mrs. Allen closed the window. Lilly Etta knew what that meant. She scuffed her tennis shoes as she walked next door to her apartment building and went inside.

Usually she ran up the stairs, but not this time. This time she walked slowly. Until an idea struck her. The fire escape, she thought. I'll call Tanya from the fire escape. She ran up the rest of the steps. She was going to help Tanya move. Tanya always helped her do things. Now it was her chance to help Tanya.

Lilly Etta rushed into her apartment and was almost to the window before her mother stopped her.

"Where you going so fast? Did you touch your ears?"

"I have to call Tanya from the fire escape! So she can ask her mother if I can come over and help her move."

"How about helping me wash greens? They're

in the sink now, Lilly Etta. You can spray them."

"But I want to call Tanya. I want to help her move!"

"Don't call Tanya. You can't help her."

"Why? Mrs. Brown won't care."

"She'll care. They're not moving, Lilly Etta. They're in trouble."

"Trouble? They're not in trouble. They're moving!"

"No, Lilly Etta. They're being put out. Those men going to pile their furniture on the sidewalk and leave it. When you got seven children, it's not easy to pay rent. Sometimes there's no money." Mrs. Allen spoke softly to her daughter. "Don't go over Tanya's."

Lilly Etta stood very still. She had seen people being put out before. It couldn't happen to Tanya. "If it stays on the sidewalk," she managed to say, "someone will steal it. People will steal Tanya's stuff."

"Nobody will steal it."

"Yes they will. Remember Mr. Larry? Remember when they piled his stuff on the sidewalk? Everybody stole it. Everybody! If anyone steals Tanya's stuff, I'll die." Lilly Etta sat down on the kitchen chair. "I'll die."

"It was different with Larry. Larry was an old man. He told people to take it because he wasn't coming back."

"No he didn't!" Lilly Etta was screaming. "They sneaked and took it. They sneaked!"

"Nobody sneaked. They took it after a few days. They thought his relatives would want it, but nobody came. Larry went to the country to live and would never use or need any of it again. Other folks needed those things right then. Nobody sneaked."

"When Mrs. Ruth's stuff was put out, the police and newspaper people and television people and the cameras came, and they had to put all her stuff right back in the house. Why don't they come and make them put Tanya's stuff back in the house too? Maybe Tanya will get a lot of new things like Mrs. Ruth got. Chairs and beds and everything. Money too."

"That was different, Lilly Etta. It was a mistake to put Ruth out. She was old and blind and crippled and her checks were stolen twice, so it was a real news story."

Lilly Etta thought about that for a while. It didn't make sense. Maybe it wasn't any news story, but it was a mistake to put out Mrs. Brown too. How could they put out a lady with seven kids? A lady who sang so good! Lilly Etta thought Mrs. Brown had the best voice in the corner church. Especially if she was singing with her eyes closed. Yes, Lilly Etta decided, it was just as bad to put out Mrs. Brown and Tanya and all the other children as it was to put out Mrs. Ruth.

But while she was spraying greens she decided something else. "It doesn't matter any more about people taking Tanya's stuff, because we can put it in our house. The whole pile can fit in our house."

"We got no room."

"Yes we do. We can put some of it in the hall and some in me and the twins' room and some in your room. And a whole lot can fit in the living room!"

"Be careful with that spray. You getting water all over the floor."

"Can't we, Mamma?"

"No. We can't bring her things in here."

Lilly Etta looked at her mother. Then she spoke quietly. "Aren't you going to help Mrs. Brown? She's your friend."

"Yes. I'm her friend and I been her friend for years." Mrs. Allen touched the neckline of her large-flowered dress and stood still for a moment before she started peeling potatoes again. "But I can't help her. She knows I can't help her." It was very quiet in the small kitchen.

After a time, Lilly Etta pushed her braids back and started again to spray cold water on the curly green leaves that filled the sink.

Then there were two sounds in the kitchen. One was the sound of potatoes plopping into water. The other sound was of water lightly gushing from a hose onto wet, crisp leaves.

There was one other sound, but you couldn't hear it. You had to see it. Lilly Etta was crying.

Her tears ran down and mixed with the hose water and the shiny greens.

"You sure nobody will steal Tanya's stuff?" she whispered. "You sure?"

The tears made her lips slippery but Lilly Etta spoke carefully. "If I see anybody stealing it, I'll call the police. I'll call the newspaper people and the television people with the cameras. I'll tell them who I saw." A violent spray of water almost flooded the sink but Mrs. Allen said nothing. "I'll tell!"

Lilly Etta turned the water off, unscrewed the hose

9

from the faucet, let the water drain from the long rubber tube, wrapped it into as small a circle as she could, and dumped it into the large roasting pan where it stayed when not in use. It was the same hose her mother used to wash Lilly Etta's hair.

"When I get big," she whispered, just loud enough for her mother to hear, "I don't want friends that can't help me!"

Then she ran from the kitchen, through the hall into the living room, and straight to the front window. She looked down at the street, which was now very crowded. People were watching the men pile the furniture up.

The pile was getting longer. It looked like a sidewalk island of many colors.

Lilly Etta saw the fluffy twin beds that she and Tanya had slept on when she spent the night with her friend. They had jumped back and forth on them. She. And Tanya. And Tanya's six sisters and brothers.

She saw the blue-striped pillows they had thrown around the apartment. One had split and Mrs. Brown had gotten angry.

Lilly Etta started crying again. The tears rolled

down her face, and her throat had a large lump in it that hurt. She was trying to swallow it away and didn't hear her mother come into the room.

"Lilly Etta Allen! I'm tired of this crying business. Crying don't help nothing except when there's dirt in your eye. Now stop it."

Mrs. Allen pulled her daughter against the large-flowered dress. She smelled warm to Lilly Etta.

"Crying don't help nothing and it don't get nothing unless you going to get it in the first place." The woman twisted the girl's braids gently and pushed the straw in her left ear back and forth carefully. "I can't help them, Lilly Etta. The city says this can't go in my house and that can't come in my house, and I have to listen. Or else there'll be no money for us. How can I buy those real gold earrings if I have no money?"

The lump in Lilly Etta's throat was getting smaller, but she didn't want to talk.

"I got to take care of us first. Louise Brown knows that. That don't mean we're not friends. Friends ain't just to help each other."

Lilly Etta wanted to sink into the wonderful blackness of her mother, but she didn't know how. So she hugged her and stopped crying.

"All I got is you, the twins, this small apartment, and a little check each month. I can't do nothing to bring us trouble."

One of the twins walked into the living room, knocked over a hassock, then saw his mother and sister standing close, and squeezed in between them. When he noticed Lilly Etta's face, he pulled her arm.

"Why you crying, Lilly?" he asked. "Why you crying?"

"I'm *not* crying," she said and moved away. He followed.

"See! You crying. See!"

"Stop following me! And shut up." Lilly Etta wanted to scream. She did. "Every time I turn around, you're following me. Make Greg stop following me, Mamma!"

"You get a spanking, Lilly? You get a spanking?" he persisted.

"Get away from me! Go on back to sleep—or something!" she yelled.

Mrs. Allen was shaking her head. "You got no reason to holler like that, Lilly Etta. You can't take Tanya's trouble out on him."

The boy moved close to his mother but kept watching his sister.

Lilly Etta watched him too and felt sorry that she had yelled. But nothing was going right today. Tanya was in trouble. She was being put out because she wasn't a real news story like Mrs. Ruth.

But maybe she was.

Lilly Etta had the beginning of an idea. Her mother couldn't do anything to help. But maybe Lilly Etta could. She and Tanya together. But she would need money for it to work. In her crayon box she had fifteen cents she'd saved to buy pencils. It would be a start. But she needed an excuse to go outside.

Lilly Etta glanced at Greg, who was still standing close to their mother, and suddenly knew what to do. She walked over and picked her brother up. "You want to go outside?" she asked and tickled him. "Just you and me. I'll let you ride on the rusty tricycle in the basement—"

"It don't have no wheels to ride."

"You can still ride it," she said, turning toward her

mother, who was looking out the window. "Is it O.K. if we go outside while Gary is sleeping?"

"Good. Because this boy is only going to wake him up, and I'll never be able to cook dinner in peace." Mrs. Allen got a cloth and washed Greg's face. "Sit on the stoop, you two, till I call you."

Lilly Etta rushed to find a sweater for her brother, got the two coins from her crayon box, and pulled Greg out the front door.

Mrs. Allen's voice followed her to the hallway. "Stay out the way of those men. Don't ask them nothing. And don't go over Tanya's house!"

Lilly Etta's heart was joyful as she raced down the steps with her brother stumbling behind. "Yes, ma'am," she yelled back. "Yes, ma'am. Yes, ma'am. Yes, ma'am!"

"Lilly Etta Allen! I'll spank the lights out of you if I catch you over Tanya's. And you won't get no kind of real gold earrings for your birthday, either. Louise Brown's got enough trouble without you in the way. Hear me?"

The girl hurried on without answering, but the trip down was slower now. Lilly Etta was wondering. But she didn't change her mind about what she wanted to do. She was going to Tanya's. And she would make those phone calls. Tanya is my friend, she thought, and I have to go. It was worth a spanking, even worth not getting earrings, to help a best friend. She yanked her brother down the steps.

"Me falling, Lilly."

"If you want to go with me you have to walk fast. I got no time for babies today."

They were finally at the front door leading to the stoop and the street. Lilly Etta wrapped her hand around the worn brass knob and flung the door wide open.

The sidewalk was very crowded. Lilly Etta saw some strangers in the crowd. People were moving around, whispering and fussing at the workmen. The pile was getting higher.

One of the men in dark suits that Lilly Etta had seen go into Tanya's building had come out. He was sitting in the shiny car behind the truck. A boy was running around the car shouting at him. "You parked at a fire hydrant. The police coming to get you!"

"You stupid," another boy told him. "That's the police too!"

"He ain't no cop!"

"He's a marshal."

But the boy kept running around the car yelling, "You not supposed to be parked by no hydrant!"

The marshal ignored the boy and the crowd of people. He sat straight and looked forward—just the way he had walked into the building.

"Why people out here, Lilly? Why they standing here?"

" 'Cause grownups like to watch people in trouble instead of stopping stuff. They say they can't help."

"Help what?"

"Hush. You don't understand anything."

"Get the tricycle, Lilly—you said I could ride."

Lilly Etta looked up at her building. Her mother was not at the window. "Come on, Greg, come on! We'll ride it later."

She pulled him up and yanked him down the stone steps. Then she ran toward the building next door and jumped the first two steps of the stoop leading into it. Tanya's building. She was moving as fast as Greg's legs could go.

"Phooey," she said as she ducked past a workman. "You're too slow, Greg!"

Lilly Etta moved her brother aside as another workman came down the steps. He was carrying an armload of clothes. His face was grim as he clumped down the wooden steps. Lilly Etta stared at Tanya's yellow raincoat hanging from the large bundle. She walked up the rest of the steps slowly.

Tanya's apartment was on the fourth floor. A piece of wood under the door held it wide open. The workman behind her walked right in without knocking.

Lilly Etta held Greg's hand, banged on the door, and waited. She couldn't just walk in without knocking. Sometimes she did. But not today.

"Who's at the door?" It was the soft, low voice of Mrs. Brown.

Tanya's sisters and brothers came running. And stumbling. One crawled.

"Hi, Terence. Hi, William Kenneth. Hi, Daryl and Lynn. Alice. Kim."

"Who's at the door?"

"It's me. Lilly Etta. Tanya home?"

"Come in, baby." The woman called, "Tanya! Lilly Etta's here!"

Lilly Etta was about to walk in when she saw Tanya sitting on the window sill of her mother's almost empty bedroom. She must have seen Lilly Etta and her brother even before they had knocked. Why hadn't she spoken to them? Lilly Etta stepped inside. She felt strange.

"Hi, Tanya," she said softly, though she didn't know why. Usually she yelled it.

"I can't have company."

"Yes you can. Your mother said—"

"I can't have company and I'm very busy."

"You don't look busy to me," Lilly Etta answered in a soft voice again.

Tanya jumped from the window sill and rushed out into the kitchen where Lilly Etta and Greg stood. "You don't know everything, Lilly Etta! You have to go home. I can't have any company today."

Lilly Etta got angry. "Phooey," she said. "Your mother said you could. I went to all the trouble of getting over here and now you—" Lilly Etta stopped.

Tanya had run back into the bedroom. She turned and screamed, "Get out of my house, Lilly Etta. I hate you. I hate you! Get out!"

Mrs. Brown came swiftly. "What's wrong? What's the matter, Tanya? I told you to stop all this crying and yelling."

18

"Lilly Etta won't go home. I can't have any company."

Mrs. Brown looked at Tanya and then glanced at the marshal, who stood by the wall. "Lilly Etta, baby, you and Greg better talk to Tanya later. She's very upset. Today's not a good day for us."

"Yes, ma'am."

Greg's hand felt very small as Lilly Etta held it. She pulled him toward the steps as Mrs. Brown walked back into her apartment through the wide-open door. "Tanya, come on in the kitchen. I told you to help me put these dishes in the boxes." Tanya stood still instead of following her mother.

Lilly Etta had walked down one flight of steps before Tanya leaned over the banister.

"Lilly Etta?"

"What?"

"You can come up if you want to."

"I thought you said—"

"You don't have to if you don't want to."

"Oh, phooey," Lilly Etta muttered. She pulled her brother back up the steps. "I wish you'd make up your mind." She ran the rest of the way to her friend.

"Can't we go to the park, Lilly? I want me a Popsicle."

"Hush!"

"You got a Popsicle, Tanya?"

"No, Greg. I don't have a Popsicle—or anything." Lilly Etta knew that Tanya was going to cry even before the tears showed in her eyes. She yanked Greg hard.

"Why don't you shut up! You get on my nerves, always begging for something."

The marshal walked past them, on his way out, and almost bumped into the boy. "You kids are in the way," he said. "Move before you get hurt."

Tanya put her arm around Lilly Etta's shoulders and steered her into the tiny hallway bathroom for that floor. "Is that Lori Gross outside? Is she looking?"

"No."

"You sure? She's going to be talking about it and showing off. You sure she's not out there, Lilly Etta?"

"I didn't see her."

"Is Karen?"

"No."

"Is—"

"Look out the window, Tanya. That's all you have to do. Mostly, it's grownups out there. Look out the—"

"No. Because people keep looking up and everything."

"Phooey on them."

Greg was knocking on the bathroom door. But neither of the girls made a move to let him in. Tanya kept leaning against the mustard-colored wall.

"They're putting us out, Lilly Etta. In front of all our friends. All my clothes and everything."

"Nobody is out there we like. None of our friends."

"But they're going to find out. They'll know."

"Don't worry about it," Lilly Etta said. "Don't worry."

"Just because my mother didn't pay the rent three times, they have to come and take everything out. She was paying part of it. She wanted to pay all of it but she couldn't. They didn't even give her a chance. As soon as everything is out they're going to lock the door. And we won't have a place to live."

Both girls were quiet. They heard Greg and the other kids running up and down the hallway.

21

"Look, Tanya, I've got an idea. Remember when they tried to put Mrs. Ruth out? The police and the newspaper people and the television people and cameras came, and they made the men put all Mrs. Ruth's stuff right back again. We'll phone them, and they'll come for you."

Tanya's eyes brightened for just a moment. Then she looked down. "They'd never come, Lilly Etta."

Lilly Etta grabbed her friend's hand. "Yes they would! We'll phone them and they'll come. I've got a nickel and a dime, but that's not enough. Do you have any money?"

"My mother has some in her box. There's always some change in there mixed up with stuff. But maybe I shouldn't take it."

"Of course not, but this is important, to help your mother. She wants us to help."

"I'm scared to take it."

"But there's no other way to get enough money to call everybody."

"TANYA! Come on, baby. I need you. Bring Lilly Etta too. She can help. The sooner this is over the better!"

"We just have to have the money to call," Lilly

Etta whispered as they walked toward Tanya's kitchen. "Or else we can't help. Get it, Tanya."

"Do you think we can really call those people?"

"Of course. We'll go to the park and use the telephone booth next to the mailbox. The broken mailbox that everybody climbs on."

"But do you think they'll come?" Tanya watched her small desk-and-chair set being carried down the steps. "For real?"

"Sure they'll come. But first we have to help your mother put the dishes in the boxes. Let's go."

The girls looked at each other for a moment and then rushed toward the kitchen. Greg and the Brown children were pushing each other in the long hallway and laughing and falling.

The dishes began to go into the boxes and bags very fast. Too fast for Mrs. Brown. "Hold it, baby," she said. "Or I'm going to have a glass mess." The girls didn't know which one she meant but they both slowed down. After a while Lilly Etta asked a question.

"Why didn't you act like you weren't home when the men came? Then they couldn't have got in."

Mrs. Brown smiled a little. "No, baby. They could

still get in because the landlord gives them a key. Pretending not to be here wouldn't make no difference."

"What about Mrs. Ruth? Her stuff was put back after all those people came. Maybe they'll come for you." Lilly Etta looked at Tanya.

"Ruth was blind. They had to help her. I'm all right and I can work. But if I don't work, I don't get any money for that day." Mrs. Brown pulled over another box. "With seven children, somebody is always sick. I can't go to work and leave no sick baby with Tanya. If I'm sick it don't matter, I go to work anyway." Alice, the baby, was taking some of the dishes back out of the boxes. Mrs. Brown moved her away. "I spend the money first for food and try to save a little for rent. Tanya knows, sometimes I have to use the rent money for food and sometimes for medicine. I got too far behind with my rent this time."

"How come you didn't go to the bank?" Lilly Etta asked.

Mrs. Brown smiled again. "The bank won't help and I can't beg. So that's that. Careful with those glasses, baby." One of her children was trying to stuff a pot into a bag already filled with glasses.

24

The girls worked faster but more carefully. Finally they were finished.

"That's it," Tanya said. "Can I go to the park with Lilly Etta for a while? Please? Just for a little while?"

"Go ahead, baby. I think you need to get out the house for a minute. But hurry back."

"Get the money, Tanya," Lilly Etta said as they ran down the hall dragging Greg. "We have to get a move on. Before Mamma calls me!"

"I don't know, Lilly Etta. My mother said they wouldn't come for her the way they did for Mrs. Ruth. I don't think it'll work."

"It'll work, Tanya. Your mother had to miss her pay because of the little kids being sick. And use the rent money for food. It's just as bad to put her out as Mrs. Ruth. But you've got to get the money. What I have isn't enough to call everybody."

"I'm scared again. I don't want to take the money."

"Oh, phooey, Tanya!"

"O.K.! O.K. I'll get it." A workman went by carrying the square pink kitchen table. Lilly Etta remembered she had just used it to hold the box she was piling dishes into. Now it was going to the sidewalk pile like everything else. It seemed strange that all this was happening to her best friend.

Lilly Etta could hear Tanya fumbling around in the wooden box. Then Tanya came running out. "I got it," she whispered. They ran down the steps, Greg behind them.

"How much did you find?" Lilly Etta asked and stepped aside for one of the movers going up.

"Only a dime."

"That's not enough, Tanya." Lilly Etta stopped on the stairs. "We need three dimes to call three places. The police, the newspaper, and television. We've only got two dimes and a nickel."

"Look what else I got." Tanya's hand held a pair of real gold earrings. Lilly Etta stared at the large golden circles.

"They belonged to my grandmother that died. Now they're mine. But I know how much you want real gold earrings, so you can keep them for me until I get my ears pierced. That way we have to see each other again, because my mother will bring me back to get the earrings. O.K.?"

"I'm afraid to take them. Mamma might find them. She'd kill me!" Lilly Etta held them carefully in the

26

palm of her hand. Greg was trying to look, but she wouldn't let him see.

"If you don't like them, you don't have to keep them for me. The ones you get will be prettier than these old things." Tanya's voice sounded sad again.

That decided the issue. "They're beautiful, Tanya. I'll keep them forever if you want me to."

Tanya grinned. "Come on, Lilly Etta. We're losing time." She ran ahead of Lilly Etta, who was still looking at the earrings. But Tanya stopped at the door. "I can't go out."

Lilly Etta closed her fingers around the gold. "Oh, phooey!"

"It's not happening to you, Lilly Etta, so you don't care. But I do. See if Lori Gross is out there."

Lilly Etta knew she had to, so she did. "She's not out there."

"Who's out there?"

"Look, Tanya, all you have to do is walk out the door talking and laughing. Nobody will say anything to you. But I've got to get to the corner before Mamma sees me!"

"I hope nobody asks me anything."

"They will if you walk out there looking sad. You

27

know how grownups are. Let's run out chasing Greg."

"You chasing me, Lilly?"

"Yeah! Run out the door, Greg. And don't stop till you get to the corner. RUN!" He did. The three of them tore down the stoop steps, past the crowd, and to the corner.

Then Tanya saw Lori Gross.

"Don't say anything to her," Lilly Etta hollered. "We're—"

"TANYA! WHAT'S YOUR STUFF DOING ON THE SIDE-WALK?"

"Oh, shut up," Lilly Etta said as they turned the corner.

"YOU THINK YOU'RE CUTE, LILLY ETTA!"

They ran all the way to the one-block city park.

"I told you we could do it!" Lilly Etta huffed and sat on a mound of grassy dirt. Greg flung himself down and rolled over. Tanya stood.

"I still have to go back," she said quietly.

Lilly Etta jumped up. "We'll worry about that later. First we have to make the telephone calls."

"Are you sure you can do it? Sound grown-up and everything?"

28

"Of course! That's nothing to do!"

"Ice-cream man, Lilly. I want me a Popsicle."

"Here, give him the extra nickel for a Popsicle or he'll be in our way and we won't be able to talk on the phone." Tanya gave it to him, and he scampered across the grass yelling after the ice-cream man.

"Who you going to call first?"

"The police."

Lilly Etta put the thin dime into the slot and dialed "O" for Operator. Tanya watched.

"May I help you?" the careful voice said.

"I want the police, please."

"Is it an emergency?"

Lilly Etta thought for a moment. "Yes, it is, please." She liked the way she said that.

"POLICE HEADQUARTERS." The voice was heavy and surrounded by busy noise.

Lilly Etta put her mouth close to the phone. "I'm in trouble and you must come and stop it."

"What's the trouble? And what is your name?"

"The men are taking my stuff and putting it on the sidewalk. If you come, they'll stop."

"Are the marshals there?"

"Yes, but—"

"If the marshals are there, there's nothing we can do. It's not a police matter."

"But I remember when—"

"Young lady, how old are you?"

Lilly Etta didn't answer. The voice came again. "We would like to help, but there's nothing we can do. I think you'd better hang up the phone." There was a click and the phone was silent.

"He didn't even try to help," Lilly Etta said. "He didn't even try. He just wanted to know if the marshals were there."

"They have to make sure everything is out and the door is locked. Then they leave. Nobody guards the furniture. All the marshals do is bring the paper and wait around until it's finished. The paper is the eviction notice. My mother was crying at first when they gave it to her."

Lilly Etta was leaning against the phone booth thinking. "We only have one dime left and that's for the newspaper people." She dialed "O" for Operator again.

"May I have the number for the newspaper, please?"

"Which paper do you want?"

"The large paper that comes out at night."

There was silence for a moment and then the operator gave her a number. She repeated it out loud so that Tanya could help her remember it.

The dime came back and she slipped it into the slot again. She dialed the number carefully because she didn't want to lose the dime by making a mistake.

A woman answered.

"May I speak to a newsman, please?"

"What kind of reporter do you want?"

"The kind that comes and takes pictures when people can't pay their rent and all their stuff is put on the sidewalk."

After a few clicking sounds, Lilly Etta heard another voice. It boomed, "City desk. Frazier speaking."

"Something is wrong and we want you to help us. Can you?"

"That depends. What's going on?"

"I didn't have any money to pay the rent because I had to buy food first, and now men are putting all my things on the sidewalk in a pile and everybody is looking. When Mrs. Ruth was put out, the police and the news people came and made them put it all back, and now we want you to come and make them put back all of Tanya's stuff. I mean Mrs. Brown's stuff. That's me. I'm Mrs. Brown."

"Where do you live, Mrs. Brown?" The voice wasn't booming any longer. It was quiet and gentle.

"In the tall house with the brand-new painted fire escape. I mean—that's not what I mean at all." Lilly Etta felt silly. She gave Tanya's address the right way.

"I don't think we can stop it."

"Yes you can," Lilly Etta insisted. "Yes you can."

There was no sound on the other end. Lilly Etta didn't want the reporter to hang up the way the police had, so she lowered her voice. "When you came for Mrs. Ruth, they had to put all her things back in her house."

Lilly Etta could tell that the voice was laughing a little. "Who did you say you were?"

"The lady named Mrs. Brown who's in trouble. Her girl is standing right here, and we want you to come and stop them from putting her stuff out."

"I thought you said *you* were Mrs. Brown. How old are you?"

Lilly Etta thought for a second and answered, "I'm fifty."

"Tell me about yourself."

Lilly Etta didn't know what to say. She whispered to Tanya, "He wants to know about me. What's he want to know about me for? That's silly!"

He heard her. "It's not silly at all. I think you're very interesting. But let's find out a few things. If you'll tell me who you really are, maybe I can help you. And maybe I can't. First you have to level with me. What's your name?"

"Lilly Etta Allen."

"Where do you live, Lilly Etta Allen?"

Lilly Etta told him. Then she said, "Can you help?"

"We can't really stop an eviction. We report it and draw attention when something is wrong. But from what you've told me, Lilly Etta, this is very ordinary."

"There's something else."

"I'm listening."

"Well, first, Mrs. Brown has seven children. Terence. And William Kenneth. Daryl and Lynn. Alice. Kim."

"And Tanya. You said she was standing there."

"And Tanya." Lilly Etta thought of what Mrs. Brown had said while they were packing the dishes. "Mrs. Brown missed work when the little kids were

33

sick, and she had to buy food with the rent money. So something *is* wrong. It's a mistake to put her out for that."

"That may be true, Lilly Etta, but it's not a real news story. It happens all the time." He paused a minute. "The only thing unusual in all this is you. How old did you say you were?"

"Nine. But when my birthday comes I'll be ten and then I'll get real gold earrings." She thought of how long she had been away from the stoop. "But maybe I won't, if I get in trouble—I got to get back to the stoop."

"Good luck," he said. "Maybe things will turn out all right for you and Tanya and Tanya's mother—Mrs. Brown."

"Thank you," Lilly Etta said sadly. She hung up the phone.

She had no way of knowing that the reporter held the phone to his ear for a long time.

"If we had one more dime, we could call the television people," Lilly Etta said. "Maybe they could help." But she wasn't so sure now that the others hadn't. The three of them started home.

When they got to their corner, Lilly Etta stopped. "You want to run again, so nobody will say anything to you?"

"No," Tanya said. "There's no use to that."

The crowd had spilled over into the street. It was noisier too. The workmen were having a hard time putting the furniture on the pile because people kept bothering them.

Nobody noticed the girls except Mrs. Allen, who was standing at her window. She made a motion to Lilly Etta to come up.

"I'll see you before we leave," Tanya said. "Take care of the earrings for me."

Lilly Etta was getting another lump in her throat, and she couldn't talk right. Her voice sounded funny. "I'll call you from the fire escape."

Tanya said O.K. and walked toward her building. Past the crowd and Lori Gross, who didn't say anything, and past workmen bringing out loads of sheets and blankets, and up the stoop and into the hall.

Lilly Etta and Greg went up the stairs next door.

"Where've you been, Lilly Etta? I've run to the window a hundred times looking for you! Did you go to Tanya's when I told you not to? Did you go in there getting in the way?"

Lilly Etta kept her hand tight around the large golden earrings and answered her mother's second question. "No," she said.

"Dinner's ready," her mother said sharply. "Go wash your hands and Greg's. Hurry up, I want to get out the kitchen and rest for a minute."

"Where you go, Greg?" Gary said.

"Went to the park. You was sleeping."

The twins were staring at each other and Gary was angry. He kept punching his brother and Greg started crying. At the dinner table they did the same thing. Mrs. Allen fussed, but Lilly Etta sat quietly, thinking of Tanya's trouble and the earrings she had hidden in her crayon box.

Lilly Etta was still eating when Tanya called from the fire escape. "I'm going, Lilly Etta! *I'm going!*"

Lilly Etta's tennis shoes couldn't get her to the window fast enough, and she stumbled and almost fell. "Tanya! I'm coming outside!" she hollered.

Tanya called again, "A cab is waiting for us. I have to go. I can't wait for you!"

"Mamma, Tanya has to go get in a cab. Can I run

downstairs and see her before she leaves? O.K.? Please? Please!"

"Go ahead. But don't run down the steps so fast. Else you'll fall and break your neck."

"Tanya! I'm coming out, right now! Wait for me!" She didn't get a chance to hear Tanya's answer because she was already running to the front door, but she thought of something and ran back to her mother. "How come you're not going down to say good-by to Mrs. Brown? And them too," she said, pointing to her brothers. "They're all the time playing with William Kenneth!"

The twins were getting away from the table. "William Kenneth outside?" Gary said. "We going outside to play with William Kenneth?"

Mrs. Allen put them back on their chairs. "You go on, Lilly Etta. Louise Brown don't need me standing around looking. I guess I told her what I had to say already." Mrs. Allen's voice was quiet.

Lilly Etta watched her for a moment before she dashed out the door. Maybe her mother didn't want to say good-by again, but she did, and she had to hurry.

The other apartments blurred as she whizzed by.

37

She didn't stop until she was standing next to Tanya on the sidewalk.

Lilly Etta didn't feel strong any more. Tanya was really leaving.

"Don't go, Tanya," she cried. "Please don't go." Lilly Etta wanted to say, You're my best friend. Nobody else except you. But she didn't.

"I have to go, Lilly Etta. I *have* to."

Lilly Etta was beginning to feel sick in her stomach. Why did Tanya's voice seem so far away?

"We're going to Cousin Helen's. But I don't want to. Every time we go over there, Steven and I end up fighting because he doesn't want anybody to touch his bike and stuff. Now we'll be fighting forever!"

Mrs. Brown was pushing her children into the taxi while she talked to a few women. Lilly Etta pulled Tanya over to her mother. "Can Tanya stay with me tonight?" she asked. "Can she, please? Maybe till you find another place to stay? She can sleep with me, and we can watch your things so nobody can take them. We'll take turns."

"No, Lilly Etta, baby. Tanya's got to go with me. I don't know what I'd do without her. Don't worry about the furniture—the Lord will find a way." Mrs. Brown rubbed Tanya's cheek. "Get in the cab. We've got to go."

Lilly Etta leaned close and whispered in Tanya's ear. "I've got the earrings in my crayon box. Don't forget to put your mother's dime back, and call me on the telephone if you can. I'll be waiting every day, so don't forget."

"No," Mrs. Brown was saying. "The other cab took all the baby things and everything else I need right away."

A woman was fussing. "Big deal," she said. "And big men. Putting seven babies and a mother on the street. Don't make no sense." She touched Mrs. Brown. "Keep your head up, Brown, this ain't no end to everything." She walked over to the pile and pointed to a highchair. "Babies on the street!"

"I'm going to do what I told you," another woman said. "My husband's people have a house they been thinking about renting. I'll see about it for you."

"How come you didn't offer it before?" someone said.

"I didn't know about this thing before now," she

snapped. "Why don't you put your money where your mouth is?"

A man walked up to Mrs. Brown and handed her some money. It was the same man that Lilly Etta had seen yell at the movers when they first arrived. "Take this for cab fare," he said.

"No." Mrs. Brown shook her head. But the man leaned in and gave it to the cab driver. "That's enough to cover it, ain't it, man?"

"Sure thing," the driver answered.

Mrs. Brown hugged the man. There were tears in her eyes.

"Grow stronger, sister," he said to her and walked away.

Everyone was talking, but Lilly Etta didn't want to talk any more and neither did Tanya. They both knew that. So Tanya sat close to the driver and stared at the steering wheel while Lilly Etta just stood at the curb. There was nothing left to do or say.

The cab pulled away and moved slowly down the crowded street.

Lilly Etta waved until it disappeared and then ran up her stoop, into the hallway, and up to her apartment. She pushed the door open and then slammed it shut, which her mother didn't like. Then she ran to the front window and yanked it open.

The crowd was moving away but not as fast as Lilly Etta wanted. She yelled, "Stop looking, everybody. Go away! Go away! You didn't try to help, so go away!" Nobody paid any attention to her because she really didn't yell it very loud, and she was three floors up. Lilly Etta closed the window. "I'm not looking, Tanya. Nobody can make me look. Nobody. And everything will be all right too because I'll help you. I'll help you even if I never get real gold earrings of my very own." Lilly Etta was crying. Tears fell down her face, around her nose, and under her chin. "I'm going to stay up all night and watch your stuff!"

Later that evening, Lilly Etta looked down at the pile for the hundredth time. Everything was still in place. Except for some magazines. Pages and pages were flapping in the wind.

Wind?

Where had the wind come from all of a sudden? Lilly Etta wondered. It hadn't been windy all day. She saw that it was darker than it should be.

Lilly Etta looked up. The sky looked funny. Like rain. RAIN!

"*Rain!*" she yelled to her mother. "I think it's going to rain. It's windy and everything and the sky is too black and it's too dark outside." She could hardly say the words. "You think it's going to rain, Mamma? It's not going to rain, is it?"

"Now listen, Lilly Etta, even if it does, there's nothing you can do about it."

"But it can't—it just can't. Everything will get all wet. Then it won't be any good!" The girl ran to the living-room table where the newspaper was kept. "I'll read the weather report! It's on the front page. At the top."

The table was empty. Lilly Etta ran back to her mother. "Where's the newspaper?"

"Next door. Bertha borrowed it."

"Oh, phooey! Why can't she buy her own newspaper? When I need it, it's not here!"

"That's enough, Lilly Etta."

"But I've got to know if it's going to rain."

Mrs. Allen shook her head at her daughter. "I don't know about the rain." She walked into the children's bedroom. "Nobody knows about the rain."

"Miss Bertha, next door, knows about the rain. She's got our newspaper." Lilly Etta held her mother's arm and rubbed it. "I'm going to get our paper," she said carefully.

"You're not."

"How come? It's our newspaper."

"Leave my arm alone. I said you're not going over there bothering her. You can't change the weather, anyway. Go take your bath."

Lilly Etta walked into the bathroom mumbling. "It's dumb to lend the newspaper when somebody wants to know the weather report."

She was still mumbling when she climbed out of the tub. She dried herself quickly, stumbled into her pajamas, wiped the tub clean, and ran out of the bathroom, straight to the living-room window.

Lilly Etta opened the window and leaned halfway out, staring at the sky. Her mother came up behind her, pulled her away, and slammed the window shut.

"Looking won't help," Mrs. Allen said as she re-arranged the curtains. "Either watch that silly show you like on television or go to bed. It's time for you to go anyway. And don't let me catch you near that window again."

"But Mamma, what about Tanya's stuff?"

"No more talking about it, Lilly Etta. No more. If it rains, it rains. Nobody can stop it. There's nothing you can do."

"But Mamma—"

"I've had enough, Lilly Etta, of listening to you all day. Crying and running back and forth and even leaving the stoop when I told you not to. It's over. What's out there is out there. Just forget about it."

But Lilly Etta couldn't forget about it. She kept sneaking to the window to watch for rain until it stuck and she couldn't close it. Her mother yanked the window and yanked Lilly Etta too. The next minute she found herself in bed.

Everything had failed. Not just the telephone calls but everything. She hadn't helped Tanya at all. Lilly Etta fell asleep listening for rain.

But it was the rumble of thunder that woke her up.

Lilly Etta lay very still. She wondered if she had really heard it. There was no sound now. She had to get to the window and see what was happening.

She got out of bed slowly. If she wasn't quiet she would wake the twins. The bunk ladder squeaked and moved a little, but she didn't make a sound as she tiptoed into the living room and opened the window.

She stuck her head out. The air was hot and sticky. It was so black she couldn't see anything. Then a flash of lightning forked across the sky, making the colors in the pile visible. The crash of thunder was so loud it seemed to split the heavens open.

"Oh!" Lilly Etta stood still. "*Oh!* It's going to rain!" She almost said it too loud. She shut the window fast but quietly.

Lilly Etta went back to her room, pulled on her bathrobe, and slipped her feet into her tennis shoes. Then she tiptoed to the closet where the towels and sheets and blankets were kept. She filled her arms with as many sheets and blankets as she could carry. Even some old baby blankets. "I hope this can cover all of Tanya's stuff. But if it rains too hard . . ." Lilly Etta didn't want to think about that. She was ready to go.

Her heart was pounding and her arms hurt as she walked down the hall, past her mother's bedroom, past the bathroom, past— She heard her mother cough.

Lilly Etta waited until she could no longer hear a sound. I've got to hurry, she thought as she stood at the dark front door.

She managed to stick her arm out from the huge bundle. "I'll leave the lock off," she whispered. "I can't go back to get my key now."

The hallway was dark because the light hadn't been fixed yet. The steps squeaked loudly. Strange-sounding night squeaks.

Squeeeeeeeeeeeeaaaaaaak!

Squaaaaaaaaaaaaaaaaaaack!

Squeeeeeeeeeeeeeeeeeeeeeeeeeeak!

Lilly Etta heard laughter in one of the apartments she passed. And almost stumbled on a cat. It made her feel like she was in a ghost movie.

She and the bundle got to the ground floor, but she had to struggle to open the door. Then she almost fell down the stoop steps.

Lilly Etta tried to spread the sheets and blankets over the pile.

It wouldn't work. She couldn't reach the top in some places. And when she threw a sheet or blanket up, the wind blew it off. Baby blankets were blowing all over the street and she had to run for them.

Tucking sheets and blankets under things didn't help. Sometimes a whole blanket would disappear in a hole and not cover anything. The wind would blow the loose ends.

Blankets were sliding off and flapping in the air. Lilly Etta had to keep running around and around the pile to straighten them out.

The wind settled for a few moments and nothing moved. The sheets and blankets were still. Lilly Etta thought of something.

Quickly she climbed atop the pile. Twice she slipped because things kept moving beneath her. Something was sticking her in the leg and something else pressed against her stomach. It felt lumpy. But finally Lilly Etta found a good spot. It was on top and almost in the middle of the pile. It felt smooth and safe.

Lilly Etta stretched out her arms and legs to hold the sheets and blankets down. It took some moving around and some pulling every time the wind blew hard, but it worked.

The street was quiet. Lilly Etta began to get sleepy.

She closed her eyes and whispered, "I'll just shut my eyes for a minute. When the wind stops, I'll sneak back in the house."

The wind kept blowing a blanket against Lilly Etta's face. It felt soft and feathery against her skin. Just like someone was gently touching her. Like her mother had when she'd had a fever once.

Lilly Etta was thinking about this when she fell asleep.

"OH, PHOOEY!" was what she said when she woke up. "I'm in trouble."

The whole block was noisy and crowded, just the way it had been that afternoon. But this time there were police cars with great blinking lights and sirens.

Lilly Etta, wet and sleepy, was being lifted down from the pile. Over by the police cars she heard a man yelling, "Why didn't you bring that thing earlier? You people knew it was going to rain, but you wait for a crowd before you do something, and then you try to act like you were going to do it all the time. Yeah! I know how you think!"

Lilly Etta, wrapped in the light-tan raincoat that

had covered her when she awoke, leaned against the man who had lifted her from the pile, and mumbled, "I was only trying to help. I didn't want the rain to get on Tanya's stuff."

"Well, Lilly Etta, I think you got what you wanted," the man said.

"How come you know my name?" she said sleepily.

"You told me," he said.

Lilly Etta knew she had never seen him before in her whole life.

"Frazier. City desk. Remember?"

"You came and brought all these people to help Tanya?" It was raining hard now, but people still crowded around. Lilly Etta saw her mother coming down the stoop.

"Your telephone call stayed on my mind all day, and even though I was tired from working late tonight, I decided to come by and check out your story. Then I found you asleep on that pile in the rain." He winked. "And I thought, This is really something! So I put my coat over you and went to call my office. I told them to get over here with cameras. You were quite a sight asleep in the rain, holding down those blankets to keep Tanya's stuff dry. Tanya is your friend's name, right? The one with you when you called?"

"I never thought you'd come. I thought—" Lilly Etta saw her mother pushing through the crowd.

"People came because of you, Lilly Etta. Look over there. Do you know what that is?"

"No, sir."

"That's a tarpaulin the police are covering Tanya's stuff with. No rain will get on it any more. I've got a cop-friend named Bud at the Seventy-seventh Precinct. He brought the tarpaulin. I told the office to call him because he sort of owed me a favor." Lilly Etta liked this man's smile.

"Lilly Etta Allen! I'm going to spank the lights out of you! Look at all my sheets and blankets and things on the ground and everywhere—and wet too. And you're soaked! I can't sleep in peace without someone knocking on the door telling me what you did. Coming out here in the middle of the night waking people up and causing the police to come!"

"Yes, ma'am."

"Yes, ma'am nothing!" Mrs. Allen said just as three

men walked up. There were large camera bags swinging from their shoulders.

"Hey, Frazier," one of them said. "Is she the one who tried to cover the pile?"

"Yep!"

"How'd you happen to be here?"

The reporter glanced at Lilly Etta and smiled. "I'll let her tell you."

And Lilly Etta told them. She told them about Tanya and how she was her very best friend and about how they got the money for the telephone calls and about Miss Bertha having the newspaper and how heavy the bundle of blankets and sheets were and how dark the hall was.

"Were you afraid?"

"Of course not," she said as flashbulbs began to go off. "All I was going to do was cover the pile and go back in the house, but the wind kept blowing everything and I had to hold them down. The sheets and blankets and stuff." She didn't dare look at her mother.

The photographers took pictures of the pile and of Lilly Etta back up on it. And of Lilly Etta yawning.

51

They had to take the pictures fast because it was pouring and everybody was getting wet.

Lilly Etta watched the police and the people and the blinking patrol-car lights and Mr. Frazier. But mostly she watched her mother. "Now I'll never get real gold earrings for my birthday," she said almost to herself.

One of the reporters heard her. "How long have your ears been pierced?" he asked.

"A long time," Lilly Etta said. "All I do is get different straws all the time. Mamma burns the ends to get the germs off."

"I see."

Lilly Etta thought of the large golden earrings hidden in her crayon box, but she couldn't tell anyone about them.

"When is your birthday, Lilly Etta?" Mr. Frazier asked.

"Oh, phooey. It's a long time away. It takes a long time to be ten."

"Lilly Etta! I'm as angry as I can be with all this trouble." Mrs. Allen was wiping the rain from her face and reaching for Lilly Etta. "So just you be quiet. I don't want to hear 'phooey.' "

"ALL RIGHT! CLEAR THE AREA! GO BACK TO YOUR HOMES. IT'S ALL OVER. CLEAR THE AREA!"

Some older kids were cupping their hands around their mouths and yelling the policeman's order all over again.

"Good night, Lilly Etta Allen," Mr. Frazier said. "You're quite a girl."

Lilly Etta's mother almost dragged her up the steps to the apartment. "You just get on upstairs and get to bed," she said. "Do you know what *time* it is, girl?"

Lilly Etta was in bed, it seemed, one second after her mother opened the door. The lock was still off but her mother hadn't noticed. She had used her key.

Mrs. Allen went back down to get her sheets and blankets.

As soon as Lilly Etta heard her leave she got up, reached into her closet for the crayon box, and pulled out the earrings. "Maybe you brought me good luck," she whispered. "There's a cover on the pile, and the police and the reporters came just like they did for Mrs. Ruth. Now all Tanya's stuff will go back in her house. I just know it!" Lilly Etta put the crayon box back and ran to lock the door. Then she climbed up to her bunk and fell asleep right away. Even before she could turn over.

She didn't see her mother, later, standing by her bed with an armful of wet sheets and blankets. Mrs. Allen was smiling and shaking her head.

The morning and evening newspapers printed the story with pictures. Lilly Etta saw her face and the pile of blowing blankets and sheets.

There were some questions she wanted to ask her mother but she thought it best to stay out of her way. She hadn't had a spanking yet and she didn't want one.

That evening when the Allen family sat down to dinner the doorbell rang. "I knew it," Mrs. Allen said. "Every time I sit down someone rings!" She went to the door. "Who is it?" she called.

"*Police.*"

"Oh, my goodness. The police again. All because that child won't listen!"

"No trouble this time. It's something good. We'd like to talk to Lilly Etta."

"Come in. LILLY ETTA!"

"Yes, ma'am?"

"Come in the living room and bring the twins with you. Hurry up. The police want to talk with you."

"And a reporter." Lilly Etta recognized Mr. Frazier's voice and she was glad. Now she could ask the question that was bothering her each time she looked out the window.

"What you doing, Lilly Etta? Hurry."

"I'm coming," she yelled. She came into the living room pulling one of the twins and asking the question. "How come the police and the newspaper people didn't make the men come and put Mrs. Brown's furniture—you know, Tanya's stuff—back in the house like before when you came for Mrs. Ruth? All day long I've been looking outside and it's still there!"

"Hi, Lilly Etta. Everything's going great for Mrs. Brown. And you did it!" Mr. Frazier lifted her up. "Not the police or newspaper people."

"Telephones have been ringing all day," the policeman added. "A warehouse has offered to store her things for free for a while. They'll pick up the furniture tonight. She's had a job offer, and a nursery school has agreed to keep her children for a small fee so she can work. And there's a larger apartment right here in the neighborhood which I understand she's going to rent."

"It looks like you're going to get your Tanya back, Lilly Etta Allen," said the man in the light-tan raincoat.

"I'm so glad," Mrs. Allen said. "I'm so glad for that family." Mrs. Allen had tears in her eyes, just a little, but Lilly Etta could see them. She wasn't afraid, because she knew her mother was crying because she was happy.

"And we have something for you too, Lilly Etta. Something you want." Mr. Frazier put her down and handed her a box. "Open it," he said.

Lilly Etta did. And then she couldn't believe her eyes.

The box was filled with earrings.

Real gold earrings and some silver ones too. Lilly Etta had never seen so many in her life.

"Oh, Mamma. Look. Look, Gary and Greg!" The girl hugged the reporter. "Are all these mine? Can I keep them?"

The reporter smiled at her. "Yes," he said. "A lot

of people thought a little girl like you shouldn't be without earrings. They called the paper saying, 'Where can I send some earrings for the little girl in pajamas with straws in her ears?' "

"People called the police stations too," the policeman said. "So we gathered all the earrings and brought them to you."

"My goodness!" Mrs. Allen said.

"I can't wait till Tanya sees this box!"

After the men had gone, Lilly Etta remembered the hug Mr. Frazier had given her as he left. And she found it hard to eat her dinner.

The box of earrings stayed by her plate. And on the sink while she washed and dried the dishes.

"Put all the earrings in," she told her mother when the kitchen was finally cleaned up. "It won't take long."

"No, indeed. Your ears will get sore. Who ever heard of trying on as many earrings as that?"

"Phooey, then."

"Say that word one more time—and you won't try on *any!*" But Mrs. Allen was opening the box and spreading out earrings.

"Yes, ma'am."

"Just pick a few and I'll put them in."

"A *few!*"

"A few."

Lilly Etta picked a round pair, a flat pair, a heart-shaped pair, and one pair of tiny gold crosses.

Mrs. Allen put in one of each in turn.

Lilly Etta laughed to see a round earring on one side and a flat one on the other side.

But that night Lilly Etta got up once again and stayed up a long time.

She tried on every single earring. Including the pair she was keeping for Tanya in the crayon box.